The Pirate
AND OTHER ADVENTURES OF
Sam & Alice

by Akemi Gutierrez

Houghton Mifflin Company

Boston 2007

For Gabriel, Kahlil, and Torin.
And for their sisters, Alina, Maya, Aliya, and Dara

www.houghtonmifflinbooks.com

The text of this book is set in Sassoon.
The illustrations are gouache on watercolor paper.

Library of Congress Cataloging-in-Publication Data
Gutierrez, Akemi.
The pirate and other adventures of Sam and Alice / written and illustrated by Akemi Gutierrez.
p. cm.
Summary: Sam and his little sister Alice find new ways to have fun playing together.
Contents: Space patrol—The genius crocodile—The pirate.
ISBN-13: 978-0-618-73737-6 (hardcover)
ISBN-10: 0-618-73737-5 (hardcover)
[1. Brothers and sisters—Fiction. 2. Play—Fiction.] I. Title.
PZ7.G9842Pir 2005
[E]—dc22
2006009822

Printed in China
WKT 10 9 8 7 6 5 4 3 2 1

Contents

Space Patrol

Sam was packing his backpack when Alice
walked into his room with a new friend.
"Hi, Sam," said Alice. "This is Tula."

"And Tula is . . . ?"

"A PLATYPUS!" Alice laughed.
"They lay eggs!"
    "I don't have time to play," said Sam.
"I'm on space patrol. I've got orders to
see if Planet Blurg has hostile aliens on it."

Tula handed Sam an egg.
"What's this for?" Sam asked.
"Tula wants to know if we
can go with you," explained Alice.

"You can be copilot," Sam said to Alice.
"Can Tula be science officer?" asked Alice.
"Sure," said Sam. The spaceship began to
rumble louder and louder, then . . .

BLAST OFF! It was a rough and shaky ride.

The spaceship glided past many planets.
"Oooo," exclaimed Alice. "Can we land
on the pretty pink planet?"
"Nope," said Sam. "Planet Blurg is right ahead."

Tula handed Sam another egg.

"Now what?" asked Sam.

"Tula says the pink planet is safer than Planet Blurg," said Alice.

"Nah," said Sam. "There's nothing to worry about."

After the spaceship landed safely,
they tested the planet's gravity.

Sam found an unusual
carving on a boulder.

Tula made friends with some natives.

And Alice fed bread crumbs to friendly wildlife.

They started to head back to the spaceship when
a monster jumped out of a crater and grabbed Sam.
"HELP!" screamed Sam.

Tula reached into her space pack and pulled
out an egg.
"UGH!" Sam shouted. "Not now, Tula!"

But Tula gave the egg to the monster, not Sam.
The monster dropped Sam, sniffed the egg with its
sticky nostrils, then skipped away.

"What just happened?" asked Sam.
Tula handed Sam an egg.
"The natives told her that the monsters love eggs," Alice explained.

"Lucky for us that Tula made new friends,"
said Sam. "We'd better hurry back to the ship
before any more of them turn up."

"Can Tula come with us on the next space patrol?" asked Alice.

"Yup," said Sam. "I want Tula aboard every time we go to outer space."

And Tula was.

The Genius Crocodile

"I wish I knew a genius who could do my homework for me," said Sam.

"The genius crocodile could do it," laughed Alice. "But he doesn't like cheaters, so he'd only EAT your homework."

"I wouldn't waste his brain
on homework," said Sam.
"I'd rather have the genius
crocodile invent rocket-powered skates."

"I think the genius crocodile could improve production at my stand," said Alice.

"Nah, he's smarter than that," said Sam.
"Supersuction boots would be a better invention."

"I wonder if the genius crocodile could make a soap bubble that doesn't pop," said Alice.

"No, no," said Sam. "The genius croc could create a force field around me so I'd never have to take a bath again!"

"Maybe he would show me how to meet new friends," said Alice.

"Well, there's one thing I can invent," said Sam.
"A PB&J Slippy Sloppy sandwich."

"What would you like to invent?" asked Sam.
"I wish I could invent a real person who would
play tea party with me instead of my toys," said Alice.

"One lump or two?" asked Alice.
"Better make it three," said Sam.

The Pirate

Sam and Alice were exploring the public library
when they found a mysterious map hidden behind
some books. A note was written on it . . .

If it's treasure that you seek
It's hard to find
It's hard to keep
Beware of one who lies in wait
The gold is his alone to take.

"Don't worry about the note," said Sam. "It's just to scare off treasure hunters like us."

Sam and Alice never turn down an adventure, so they sailed their little boat to the island on the map.

They followed the map's directions to a weird-looking tree.

And then to an old statue.

Which led them to a dark cave.

"Are you sure the map wants us to go in there?" asked Alice.

"Yup," said Sam. "The treasure is somewhere inside."

Sam pulled an electric lantern from his backpack.
"Why did you bring marbles?" asked Alice.
"That's my best marble collection," said Sam.
"I never travel overseas without it."

Sam and Alice walked deeper into the cave,
and Sam shone the lantern around a rocky corner.
"YO HO HO!" crowed Sam.

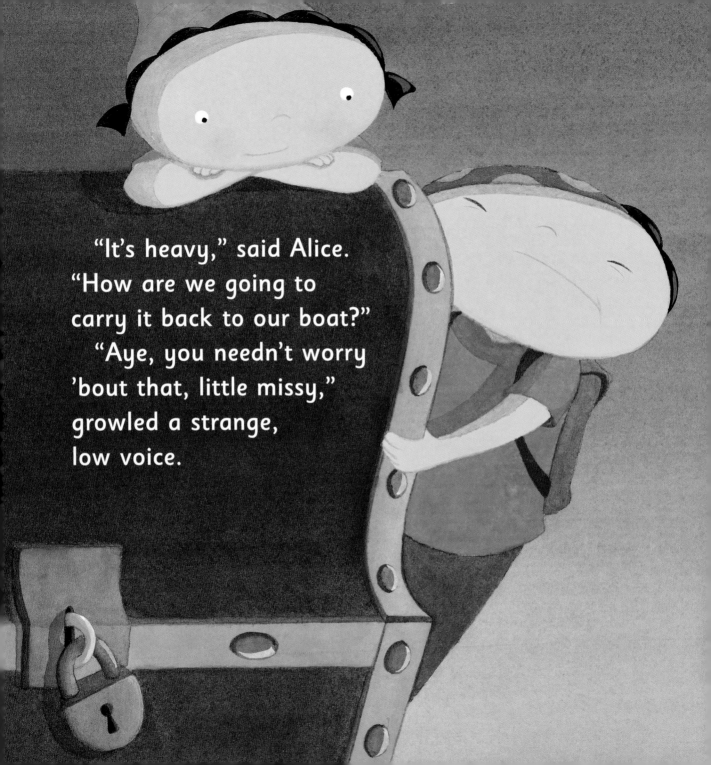

"It's heavy," said Alice. "How are we going to carry it back to our boat?"

"Aye, you needn't worry 'bout that, little missy," growled a strange, low voice.

Sam and Alice turned to see a big, mean pirate.
"The note on the map was right!" Alice gasped.
"Who are you?" Sam asked.

"Dead Eye Dirk be my name," said the pirate. "Watchin' these shores for many a year, have I. Waitin' for the scurvy wretch who'd lead me to that treasure. And so y'have."

Dead-Eye Dirk picked up the treasure chest with
one arm and slung Sam and Alice in the other.
"What are you going to do with us?" asked Sam.

"Well, I got me treasure," said Dead-Eye Dirk.
"That's all a pirate needs."

"But I can't risk you two blabbing 'bout me booty."
The pirate frowned. "'Tis a shame, but you'll both
have to walk the plank . . . and ladies first."

"Any last words, missy?" asked Dead-Eye Dirk.
"Yes," said Alice. "When are we having lunch?"

"LUNCH?" Sam and the pirate asked.
"I'm hungry," Alice complained, pouting.

"I have some cookies in my backpack," Sam said.
But he poured out his marble collection on the
deck instead and pulled in the plank.
 "BLAST THESE CURSED VARMINTS!" yelled the
pirate, slipping and sliding on the marbles.

Sam and Alice grabbed a mop and pushed the pirate off the ship. And Dead-Eye Dirk fell into the drink, marbles and all.

Sam and Alice opened the treasure chest and found gold and jewels.

"Can we have lunch now?" asked Alice.

"Aye, little missy," growled Sam. "With this treasure, we'll buy a feast fit for the queen of England herself!"

"So is your tuna sandwich good?" asked Sam.
"ARRRR, it's good!" replied Alice.

The End